Seamus Ó Conaill

SPUDS
AND THE
SPIDER

ILLUSTRATED BY
Daniele Archimede

GILL BOOKS

Spuds Potsofgold was a happy leprechaun … most of the time. He loved his home, Toadstool Cottage, which sat at the end of a rainbow and had its very own wishing well.

He lived with his leprechaun wife, Rose Goodytwoshoes, and a teeny tiny field mouse called Steve, who meowed because he thought he was a cat.

In fact, there was only one thing that made Spuds upset.

Spuds hated spiders.

He hated their loooong, **scratchy** legs …

Their googly black eyes that swivelled and **popped** …

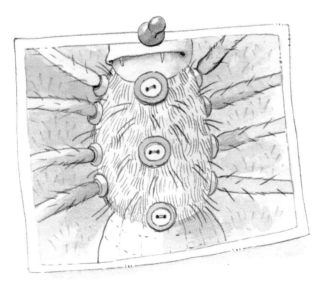

And their hairy bodies that **tickled** when they touched.

There was one particular spider he hated
most of all. And that was the one living in a
corner of Toadstool Cottage.

Leggers McWeb was the spider's name.
Leggers liked making webs, writing
poetry for lady spiders and eating juicy
flies for dinner.

How they **squished** and **crunched!**

Every night, when Spuds, Rose and Steve were asleep, Leggers would wake up. He'd slip out of his little home – a crack in the toadstool wall – and weave an almost invisible thread from rafter to rafter, from window to door, over the fireplace and up the walls.

Every morning, when Spuds would get up, webs and threads would stick to his face and neck.

'That Leggers! I'll **crush** him, I'll **stomp** him, I'll **mash** him!' he would exclaim.

Of course, Leggers never heard a word. He was fast asleep, his tummy full of flies.

Spuds would get out his feather duster and clean up all the cobwebs. He'd have to reach right into the corners, crouch down under tables, climb up into the rafters and check under the chairs.

'That spider needs a good squishing,' Spuds grumbled and groused.

'It's only a little spider,' Rose said. 'He keeps flies away from my delicious shamrock pies.'

'When I get him,' Spuds said, 'I'm going to squash him like a sponge.'

Rose shook her head and said,

He means no harm,
Let him go,
Just be kind,
You never know.

One night, Spuds stayed awake, waiting for Leggers to come out from his little hole in the wall. Poor Leggers came out, all ready for a night of webs and flies …

BAM!

'Got you!' Spuds said.

Poor Leggers was trapped under a basket. Spuds grabbed his leprechaun boot to flatten poor Leggers with his heel.

But Rose shook her head and said,

He means no harm,
Let him go,
Just be kind,
You never know.

Spuds held his boot for a minute, thinking. He knew she was right, so he put the boot down. He walked outside with the spider and tossed him into the garden.

'Promise me you'll stay outside,' he said.

Leggers nodded and scuttled off.

Although he was grateful he hadn't been smooshed by a shoe, Leggers did what spiders do.

He made webs in the garden.

Webs all across the gate, webs all over the gutters and webs all over the wishing well, where he found lots and lots of delicious flies and bugs.

The next morning, Spuds glanced out the window and saw the threads all over his garden.

'That spider. Wait till I catch him!' he exclaimed. He put on his green suit and top hat, keeping one of his boots in his hand.

In the garden, he waved his boot at Leggers. 'I'll smoosh you to smithereens!' he said, his leprechaun cheeks bright red. But Rose shook her head again.

He means no harm,
Let him go,
Just be kind,
You never know.

So Spuds let Leggers go again and Leggers ran off over the fields.

After that, all was peaceful in Toadstool Cottage. Steve the mouse (who still thought he was a cat) chased other mice in the garden. Rose made beautiful lucky pies made of shamrocks.

And Spuds did what he loved doing most – making wishes in his wishing well outside. Sitting on the edge of the well, he made wish after wish, for crocks of gold, mounds of chocolate, new boots and a new green hat for St Patrick's Day.

One day, while he wished, he leaned over just a little too far, and he slipped …

... until he landed with a SPLASH!

'Help,' he shouted up. It was such a long way!
But Rose was too busy making pies to hear
him. And Steve was busy concentrating on how
to purr (and not having much luck). There
seemed to be no one around to help him.

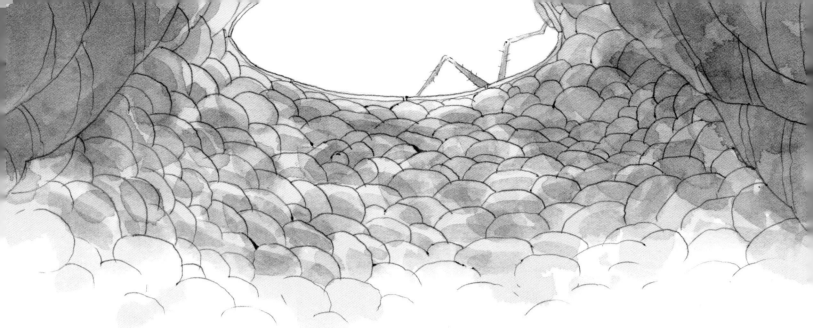

But then Spuds heard a sound above him
– a rustle in the bushes and a whooshing
through the air. A leg appeared at the top
of the well, then another, and another, and
then he saw …

... googly black eyes
and a hairy, hairy body!

'Leggers!' he said. 'Go for help. I'm stuck!' But the spider didn't run off. Instead, he began doing what he did best.

Down, down, down, came the strongest, finest piece of thread. Leggers kept making more and more, until finally the rope reached all the way to the bottom. 'Grab on!' he said.

Spuds grabbed the thread. It was a bit sticky, but very strong. Bit by bit, he began climbing and climbing.

Up and up he went, until finally the hole got bigger and bigger ... and POP! He hopped over the side and back into the sunny garden.

'My wish was answered!' he said. 'I was saved …
you saved me!' He was rather glad now he hadn't
smooshed poor Leggers.

'Of course,' the spider said.
'I may have sticky webs and beady eyes,
but I wanted to help when I heard your cries.'

From then on, Leggers was allowed into the garden to eat all the fat bugs and juicy flies he wanted.

Rose even gave him slices of shamrock pie (which he didn't like but was too polite to say).

Leggers was happy to make a bit of thread whenever Spuds wanted a lead for walking Steve, or a fishing line to catch a nice bit of trout from the nearby pond.

All was well in Toadstool Cottage.

Gill Books
Hume Avenue
Park West
Dublin 12
www.gillbooks.ie

Gill Books is an imprint of M.H. Gill and Co.

Text © Seamus Ó'Conaill 2018
Illustrations © Daniele Archimede 2018
978 0717I 7995 4

Designed by www.grahamthew.com

Printed by L&C Printing Group, Poland
This book is typeset in 21pt on 26, Mrs Eaves OT .

The paper used in this book comes from the wood pulp of managed
forests. For every tree felled, at least one tree is planted, thereby
renewing natural resources.

A CIP catalogue record for this book is available from the British Library.

5 4 3 2